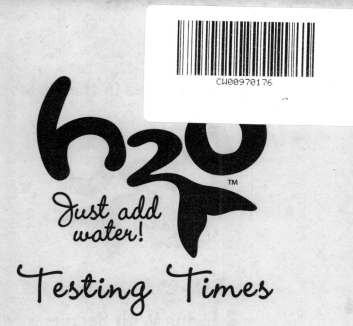

h2o ™

Just add water!

Testing Times

Read other titles in the series

1 No Ordinary Girl

2 Living With Secrets

3 Fishy Business

4 A Sleepover Tail

5 Sequins for Sea Queens

6 First Crush

7 Moonspell

h₂o

Just add water!

Testing Times

Adapted by Sue Behrent

SIMON AND SCHUSTER

SIMON AND SCHUSTER

First published in Great Britain in 2010 by Simon & Schuster UK Ltd,

1st Floor, 222 Gray's Inn Road, London WC1X 8HB

A CBS Company

Originally published in Australia in 2007 by Parragon

Licenced by ZDF Enterprises GmbH, Mainz

© A JMSP Programme in association with FFC, PFTC, Network 10, ZDF

German Television Network and ZDF Enterprises GmbH

A CIP catalogue record for this book is available from the British Library

ISBN 978-1-84738-775-2

10 9 8 7 6 5 4 3 2 1

Printed by CPI Cox & Wyman, Reading, Berkshire RG1 8EX

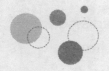
Chapter 1

Cleo watched Lewis intently as she walked along beside him. She knew she should have been listening more closely to what he was saying – something about pH and the osmotic potential of cell walls – but really she wasn't paying much attention. Instead, she wondered why Lewis always wore that old-man-style hat of his. *He looks so much cooler with his hair out*, she thought. *The way his hair falls over his eyes sometimes makes him look almost cute.* She suddenly realized what she was thinking and gave herself a quick shake. *I can't think about Lewis like that!* she thought. *He's my friend! But he* would *look much better without that hat …*

Lewis had asked her to meet him at the beach. When Cleo arrived he was already waiting there with Emma and Rikki, who were

both looking decidedly bored. Lewis had said he wanted to bring them up to date on how his research was going on the samples he'd collected from the moon-pool. He'd been running different tests on the rocks and soil and analyzing water samples. He'd also mentioned something about some news he wanted to share with them all. The way Lewis was rabbiting on though, Cleo didn't think it sounded like anything to get too excited about.

"I've been working all day every day and I think I'm getting close to figuring out what your transformation's all about," Lewis said enthusiastically, waving his arms around as they walked. He really sounded like he was on the verge of some kind of a major breakthrough, but he was telling them about it in a *very* roundabout way. Cleo didn't doubt for a second that Lewis was about to uncover something amazing, something that would change things forever, but she wished he'd get to the point sooner rather than later! *Maybe that hat stops*

2

him from thinking straight, she mused, trying not to laugh.

"Lewis, we've kind of figured that one out for ourselves," Emma said dryly.

"Yeah, for me it was the tails," Rikki agreed sarcastically. "Was it the tails for you, Cleo?"

"Ease off on Lewis," Cleo chided gently. "He's trying to help." She really could imagine him making a scientific breakthrough; maybe not now, but definitely at some point during his life. *Yes,* she thought, *Lewis is going to make a big scientific discovery that will change the world one day. And I'll be so proud of him when he does. Only right now he needs to concentrate on finding out why whenever we touch water we become mermaids!*

"*Exactly*," said Lewis, thankful for the support. At least Cleo was taking him seriously. Now he just had to convince Emma and Rikki that he was working hard on their behalf.

"Science ..." Lewis went on, stopping for

a second to think about how best to convince them that his scientific approach was the *only* chance they had of discovering what it was that had turned them into mermaids. "Science is the key that unlocks the door to the mysteries of life." He turned to take in Emma and Rikki's reaction to this profound statement. They both just yawned. "You don't much care, do you?" he said, disappointed.

"No," Rikki answered matter-of-factly.

The three girls walked on up the beach, leaving Lewis standing rooted to the spot, appalled by the lack of respect they apparently had for science. He shook his head wearily and trotted to catch up with them.

"Look guys," he said, trying again to convince them to hear him out. "In the next week or so I'm going to have an opportunity to …"

But the girls weren't listening; they walked past without even giving him a second glance.

Quickening his pace, Lewis overtook them, only to stop suddenly to prevent the girls from walking any further.

Emma and Rikki stared at him blankly, as if he was just a large, boy-shaped object that had suddenly appeared in their way. "Forget it," Lewis mumbled dejectedly.

"*Lewis*," Rikki said sternly, grabbing his shoulders and giving him a bit of a shake, "speak!"

Lewis's eyes lit up. They were going to hear him out after all!

Cleo smiled, pleased that Rikki and Emma were not only going to give him an opportunity to explain at last, but were actually prepared to listen properly!

"Okay," Lewis began eagerly. "There's someone arriving today. She's doing dolphin research at the marine park. Her name is Denman. She did her PhD at 21!" His voice almost cracked with excitement as he told them

this. He was so clearly astounded by the fact that anyone could gain a PhD at such a young age.

"Can you believe *that*?" he hooted delightedly.

"I'm tingling," Rikki replied, rolling her eyes at Emma and Cleo.

Lewis ignored her. "These days, she's one of the world's leading experts in aquatic mammalian cellular evolution. If I can tap into her research ..."

"And how are you going to get access to a scientist like her, Lewis?" Emma said, raising her eyebrows sceptically.

"I have my methods," Lewis answered mysteriously, suddenly realizing that he actually didn't have the faintest idea how he was going to get close enough to Denman for her to share her research with him. *I'll have to come up with a plan for that*, he thought, *but it shouldn't be too difficult.*

"No way!" Rikki said firmly, interrupting Lewis's thoughts. "You are *not* going to tell a real scientist about us."

"Guys, it's *me*," Lewis said pleadingly, his arms stretched wide. He really believed that Dr Denman could help them and wanted to give this plan every possible chance of success. In fact, to increase their chances he'd even been emailing Dr Denman on a daily basis in the hope that she'd give him a job as her research assistant when she arrived. Of course, there was no need to tell the girls that detail just yet – they'd probably over-react and say he should've asked them before even contacting Denman – but Lewis thought he had a fairly good chance of working with her. "I'll be careful," Lewis said. Suddenly his face took on a hurt expression. "Hey what do you mean, 'real scientist'?" he blurted.

Rikki just raised her eyebrows as if what she'd meant by 'real scientist' needed no further explanation. "You work it out,

Einstein," she teased.

"She can't know about us," Emma said more seriously.

"What if she wants to dissect us?" Rikki added, suddenly thinking of what a 'real scientist' might want to do to her.

"What if she goes public on us?" Cleo added, thinking that the entire world finding out about their mermaidness might be even worse than being dissected. She could just imagine the headlines on the day the story broke – 'Something fishy on the Gold Coast' or 'Mermaids from Outer Space' or something equally ridiculous. She could imagine her parents' reaction when they picked up the morning paper and saw a picture of their daughter staring back at them. Cleo shuddered at the thought.

Lewis realized that they were scared and that he had to find a way to reassure them that he'd handle Denman as carefully as possible.

8

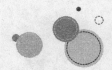

They were completely over-reacting and that was counter-productive! No, he needed calm, rational, scientific thought. He *knew* the plan could work, but he had to find a way to convince them that it was safe.

"She's a marine biologist," he explained, as if being a marine biologist made her the most trustworthy person in the world. When he saw that this had no effect on them at all he went on heatedly. "And she'll have equipment that makes the stuff at school seem like … like *toys*. If you guys want answers, I need access to that equipment, and her research."

The three girls still looked sceptical, but at least they weren't jumping up and down in a panic and leaping to irrational conclusions about what might happen. At least there was no more talk of dissection.

"So how are you going to do that without spilling your guts about us?" Rikki asked. She was far from convinced but was beginning to see that Lewis did have a point. The question of

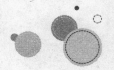

what had happened to them was a complicated one. And complicated questions sometimes needed complicated answers.

"I was thinking charm," Lewis suggested, swaggeringly slightly and dipping the brim of his hat.

"No, *seriously*?" Cleo asked.

"Come on guys," Lewis pleaded as the girls strolled past him smirking. "All I'm asking is that you *trust* me."

They'd only gone a few paces when Emma stopped.

"Okay," she said finally, turning around to face Lewis. "We *do* need to know what happened to us." She looked to Cleo and Rikki for support. They really *didn't* have any alternative if they wanted to get to the bottom of what had turned them into mermaids. They all knew that if they were ever going to learn to live with what they were, they had to have a better understanding of it.

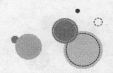

Rikki blew out her cheeks and gave a deep sigh of resignation. She knew Emma was right, but that didn't mean she had to *like* it. She looked up at Lewis and kicked at the sand beneath her feet irritably. "You'll never get to see her anyway," she huffed.

"Ah, yes I will," replied Lewis confidently, as if he had suddenly thought up a plan that would guarantee him access to Dr Denman.

"Cleo?" he asked, turning to her expectantly as if she was to play a critical part in his newly concocted scheme.

They all turned to Cleo, wondering what role she could possibly play in getting Lewis access to Denman. Cleo just shrugged her shoulders innocently. She had absolutely no idea what Lewis had in store for her.

Chapter 2

Lewis stood with his back to the laboratory wall, looking around keenly for security guards or anyone else that might catch them out. He had the *Mission Impossible* theme tune playing in his head.

Seeing that the coast was clear, he gave Cleo the signal. She looked up from where she was hiding behind a small hedge and then half-ran, half-tiptoed along the path towards Lewis, pressing herself up against the wall next to him when she got there. She was slightly out of breath with the sheer danger of what they were doing. Cleo knew that if they were discovered, she could easily lose her job.

"Lewis, we're not supposed to be in this area," she whispered.

Although he was fully aware of the huge

risk Cleo was taking by being there with him, Lewis also knew that now wasn't the time for second thoughts. Giving her a quick reassuring smile, he crept closer to the laboratory door. The restricted area of the marine park that they needed to reach was just behind the mammalian research pool, away from the action of the main dolphin display areas where they could hear the crowds cheering as they watched the two o'clock show. Lewis was counting on this being a quiet time of day around the laboratory and was hoping that everyone would be off watching the show. Everyone except Dr Denman of course.

Carefully, he swiped Cleo's security pass through the card-reader on the door, his teeth clenched in the hope that it would work – that was the one part of his plan that could have failed completely. If Cleo's pass didn't work in this area of the park, they were done for. The door suddenly clicked open with a satisfying jolt as the pass reader lit up with a green light.

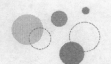

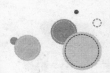

They were in! Lewis let out a long sigh of relief and warily poked his head through the crack in the door.

Finding the lab empty, Lewis squeezed himself through the doorway. Cleo followed close behind him.

"Woah, talk about heavy duty," he said, his mouth hanging open in amazement as he gazed around the room. The bench tops were groaning under the weight of expensive-looking equipment.

Cleo looked around too and although she had no idea what any of the gear was for, she was pleased that Lewis was impressed!

Maybe there is something here that we can use, she thought hopefully, forgetting for a second that if anyone caught them in the lab, they'd be in big, *big* trouble.

"What do you think she looks like?" Lewis asked absently. He picked up a small phial

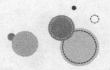

full of a strange, green liquid and held it up to the sunlight streaming in through the windows lining the upper walls of the laboratory. *What does a 21-year-old expert in aquatic mammalian evolution look like?* he wondered, realizing that he'd spoken aloud as he hastily replaced the phial in its stand.

"She spends a lot of time in the water," Cleo speculated, giving it some thought. "Maybe a prune?" she suggested hopefully.

Suddenly they heard the click of the door; someone was coming in! They'd been sprung!

Lewis felt a tight knot of fear in his stomach and for a brief moment he just stood looking dejectedly down at his feet. He didn't even want to see who had found them. *We came close,* he thought, *but not close enough. I guess now we'll just have to face the music. I only hope that Cleo thinks this was worth losing her job over. I don't want her to think that I talked her into this, even though I probably did.*

But when Lewis finally looked up, instead of seeing the burly security guards he'd been expecting, what he saw was the most beautiful woman he'd ever laid eyes on. The creature in front of him was stunning! Her long blonde hair shimmered in the sunlight and it seemed as if she was almost glowing as the light streamed in from the open door and illuminated the sides of her face.

Cleo, still standing beside Lewis, did *not* like what she saw at all.

"Can I help you?" the woman asked in a honey-sweet voice.

Lewis opened his mouth to answer, but to his considerable embarrassment, no sound came out. Instead, he just stood there opening and closing his mouth like a fish.

Eventually, as he kept moving his mouth, he started to produce some noises. Thankfully, some of them sounded vaguely like speech. "You then Dr Demon?" he stammered, getting

all the words mixed up.

"Yes, I'm Dr Denman," the woman answered with a charming smile.

"I'm Louie," Lewis said, struggling to introduce himself. "Er, Lewis McCartney," he corrected himself, reading it from the copy of his résumé he'd brought along.

"Lewis McCartney?" Dr Denman interrupted, reaching out to shake his hand. "Are you the one that sent me 48 emails about the research assistant's position?"

"Yes I am," Lewis answered happily, starting to relax as he reached out to shake Denman's hand. However much he relaxed, he couldn't stop himself from grinning at her.

"Wow," Denman said, finally retrieving her hand back from Lewis. "You must be ... very keen."

Cleo nudged Lewis's elbow, trying to snap him out of his stupor. It didn't work. Lewis just

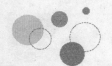

stood there grinning stupidly at Denman. *He looks like a stunned mullet*, Cleo thought.

"You're not a stalker, are you?" Denman asked jokingly.

Lewis laughed awkwardly. "Ha! Ha, a *stalker*!" he said, as if the idea was plainly ridiculous. But the suggestion did make him suddenly realize what a fool he was making of himself and he quickly remembered where he was and why he was there.

"This is Cleo," he said, remembering for the first time since Dr Denman walked into the room that Cleo was standing right next to him. He also suddenly noticed the scowl on Cleo's face.

"This is my résumé," Lewis said, leaning towards Denman and handing it to her. "If you'd like to read it," he added hesitantly.

"It's nice to meet you Cleo, Lewis," Denman replied, nodding to each of them.

"Let me say, I find your attitude ...

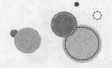

admirable," she said, searching for a polite way to describe Lewis's enthusiasm. "Science is the key that unlocks the door to the mysteries of life."

Lewis looked expectantly at Cleo, beaming at her while Denman spoke as if to say, *see? that's what* I *say.* Cleo just rolled her eyes at him and turned back to Dr Denman.

"So, mind if we take a look at what you're up to?" Cleo asked, moving closer towards the bench top nearest to her and picking up one of Denman's notepads.

"Sorry," Denman answered, taking the notepad back from Cleo and steering her and Lewis towards the door. "I'm actually at a crucial stage of something at the moment. But I will take a look at your résumé." She opened the door for them both. "Okay?"

"Okay," Lewis agreed, still in a bit of a daze as he and Cleo were ushered out. Even as the door was being closed on his face, Lewis kept

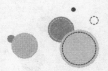

leaning his head to the side, craning his neck around to keep Denman in view for as long as possible. "Bye!" he added dreamily just before the door clicked shut.

Chapter 3

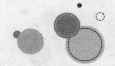

Emma and Rikki were trying hard not to laugh. They were walking through the park next to the marina and Cleo had just finished telling them all about what had happened at the marine park. Or at least, she had started to tell them what had happened, but had ended up launching into a long speech about how she thought marine biology wasn't even a real science and how anyone who spent their life as a marine biologist was really just a glorified scuba diver.

Rikki and Emma had tried to ask her whether it looked as if Lewis would get access to the lab equipment he needed, but Cleo wasn't listening. Instead, she just kept going on about how stupidly Lewis had acted when Denman walked in.

What does he think he's doing? Cleo

thought. Lewis had always told her that he preferred brunettes, like her! What was he doing drooling over a blonde like that? *She's not even* that *pretty,* she thought. *Sure, she's tall and slim and well educated, but I bet she's hideous under all the make-up she must wear.*

"Dr Denman, huh! More like Dr Baywatch Babe," Cleo scoffed. "What does *she* know anyway?"

"Well, I googled her," Emma began cautiously, knowing Cleo wasn't going to like what she was going to say next. "She wrote some important paper as part of her PhD – mutations in aquatic mammals apparently … she's got a bit of cred."

"Hmmph," Cleo muttered dismissively, shrugging her shoulders as if anyone could get a PhD. "She probably got lucky. I bet she's not even a real blonde."

Emma couldn't stop herself from laughing. She'd never seen Cleo this jealous before and

Cleo was terrible at covering it up. Emma wondered what could be causing it – it couldn't possibly have been that Cleo was *into* Lewis. Those two had been friends for ages and if something was going to happen between them, surely it would have happened by now, she thought. No, it must be something else. Whatever it was, though, Emma couldn't help but laugh.

"What?" Cleo asked innocently. "I'm just concerned about Lewis and how he's feeling right now. You should have seen him before. I mean, what if then he tells her about us?"

Emma stopped laughing immediately. The thought of Lewis telling Denman about them was a horrifying one and it sent shivers down her spine. At this stage, there was no telling whether Denman could be trusted, regardless of how much credibility she might have in the scientific community. If Denman found out about them, there was every chance that the entire world would find out. One

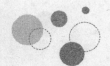

thing that Emma did know about scientists was that they were expected to publish their work, whether their findings were popular or not. That's how they all worked together, by publishing their research so that other scientists could investigate the same issue further. She couldn't imagine anyone under that much pressure deciding to keep a secret like this to themselves, no matter how ethical they might be.

Chapter 4

As soon as he'd received the news that Dr Denman had decided to give him the research assistant's job, Lewis had raced to the Juice-Net Café where he was sure that Cleo, Rikki and Emma would be hanging out. He was excited about the job and hoped they would be too. After all, as far as Lewis was concerned, this was their one and only chance to find out what had happened to them. Regardless of how much faith Cleo had in him, Lewis knew that even if he worked hard at it for the next ten years, the limited range of equipment at the school's lab meant that there was just no way he'd be able to accomplish there what he'd be able to get done in just a few days with the facilities at Denman's lab.

When he arrived at the café and saw the three girls sitting in one of the corner booths he

almost skipped over to them, he was so excited about it all. But when he sat down, squeezing himself in next to Rikki, they didn't seem so excited at all. In fact, as he started telling them all about the job and Dr Denman and how cutting-edge her research was, all he got back from them in return were some very cold and ominous glares. Emma even seemed to be grinding her teeth while he spoke.

"Plus, she's a scientist," Lewis said, adding to his list of reasons why Dr Denman was so brilliant. The comment just earned him a forceful 'hmmph' and a kick under the table from Cleo – a gentle kick, but a kick nonetheless.

"And what exactly are you going to say to her, Lewis? Are you going to ask her out for a candlelit dinner and say, 'oh, by the way, my friends got caught in a moon-pool one night on Mako Island and now they're mermaids – any idea what might have caused it?'" Emma asked when he'd finished.

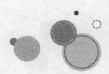

"Have a little faith, *please*," Lewis pleaded with her. "All I want is access to her lab, that's it."

"You're a sucker for a pretty face, Lewis" Emma told him sceptically. As far as she was concerned, access to Dr Denman's lab seemed like the last thing on Lewis's mind at that point.

"Pretty face?" Lewis asked incredulously, as if it was the most ridiculous idea he'd ever heard. "What, do you think I noticed whether she was pretty or not? I'm a scientist!" He made it sound as if being a scientist meant that something as mundane and work-a-day as attractiveness couldn't possibly have any influence on him. "Besides, she wasn't that special anyway," he added.

Suddenly they were interrupted by the sound of Lewis's mobile phone ringing. He looked down at the screen to see whose number it was.

"Ooh, it's her!" he said excitedly, jumping

up from the table to take the call and leaving the three girls sitting there, shaking their heads in disbelief. *What's got into him*, thought Cleo. *This is Lewis … he's normally so … so … so level-headed. I've never seen him act like … like he's got a date with Shakira or something!*

"He's got her number programmed into his phone already," she said out loud to Emma and Rikki as soon as they realized that by 'her', Lewis had meant Dr Denman. Emma reached her arm up over Cleo's back and rubbed her shoulder comfortingly.

Lewis might have left the table, but they could still hear every word he said as he strolled importantly around the café talking to Dr Denman.

"Dr Denman, how *are* you today?" they heard him say, as smoothly as they'd ever heard Lewis talk. "Uh huh, mmm," he went on casually before suddenly giggling into the phone.

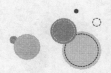

"Nervous laughter," Rikki said, watching him intently. "Not good."

"Is he *twirling his hair*?" Emma asked in astonishment. She couldn't quite believe what she was seeing.

Lewis continued to wander around the café as if he was the only person there. A couple of times, he almost bumped into the waiters, he was so oblivious to everything going on around him. He even walked straight into the pool table at one point, knocking a precariously positioned ball into one of the corner pockets and earning a fierce scowl from one of the guys who was playing. But Lewis didn't notice a thing.

"Funny, you're really funny," they heard him say as he actually jumped up onto the pool table and sat down, right in the middle of a game. The guys that were playing looked stunned for a moment and then tried to shove Lewis off, but he just went on ignoring them.

"We're in *big* trouble," Cleo said ominously, as she watched Lewis leaning back on the pool table, almost lying down on it.

"Yeah," Lewis was saying. "I'm ready to do some work experience. Any time you want me, day or night."

Cleo groaned.

"Really?" she heard Lewis say with a laugh. "I'm counting the minutes." He hung up the phone, hopped down from the pool table and practically swaggered back to their booth.

Cleo, Rikki and Emma just stared at him, unable to think of anything to say. None of them could quite comprehend the display of love-struck foolishness they'd just witnessed. *And to think I thought that Elliot had behaved absurdly*, thought Rikki, remembering when Emma's little brother had had a crush on her. *This is way worse than that. Way, way, way worse!*

"Well, I'm convinced," Emma said finally as

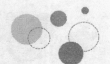
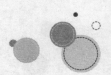

Lewis edged himself back into the seat next to Rikki. "You can't be trusted."

"*What*?!" Lewis asked indignantly, as if he had no idea what Emma was talking about.

"Lewis," Emma snapped, trying to get his full attention for a moment. "Forget about her for a minute – this is *us* we're talking about." She had to make Lewis realize that they'd put their lives in his hands. If Denman found out they were mermaids, there was really no telling what might happen. Sure, they'd all taken risks in the past and almost been caught out too, but all those risks were nothing compared to what Denman could do with the information Lewis had. "Do *not* reveal anything to her," she warned him. "Do you understand? We've got a lot riding on this."

Chapter 5

Walking through the marine park to meet
Dr Denman later than day, Lewis couldn't
help but wonder what all the fuss was about.
He was a *scientist* after all. As far as Lewis
was concerned, that meant that his motives
were absolutely pure. The only reason he was
having anything to do with Dr Denman at all
was to get answers – answers that Cleo, Rikki
and Emma needed. *He* wasn't the one that
needed the answers; *he* wasn't the one that had
gone and got himself turned into a mermaid.
Sure, maybe Denman *was* attractive, but that
just meant that he'd be enjoying a nice view
while he sought the answers they needed. Why
couldn't they understand that the only reason
he'd got himself into all of this in the first place
was for *them*?

Suddenly realizing that he'd arrived at

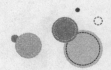

the laboratory door, Lewis shook his head, thinking that no matter how much he tried to understand girls, he never seemed to get any closer to working them out.

Gathering his thoughts and putting on his most charming voice – it didn't hurt to be charming – Lewis knocked on the door and called out, "Dr Denman."

"Lewis," he heard a gentle voice call out from behind him.

Lewis jumped slightly at the sound of his own name and turned around to where the voice had come from. What he saw almost made him lose his balance and stumble backwards into the laboratory door. Dr Denman was standing waist-deep in the research pool behind him. She was wearing a wetsuit that was half-unzipped, showing just a hint of the bikini she wore beneath it. Not only that, but she was patting a dolphin in the pool beside her, which as far as Lewis was concerned

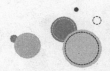

made her seem like some kind of sea-goddess.

"Hey," Denman said casually.

Lewis just stood there with his mouth agape, staring stupidly. He felt his heartbeat quicken in his chest and hoped that his cheeks weren't turning red.

"Lewis," Dr Denman said, turning to look down at the dolphin that swam happily beside her as if she hadn't even noticed Lewis's sudden inability to speak, "meet Marge. Marge is helping me out with some research too. Isn't she beautiful?" she added, stroking the dolphin's dorsal fin. Marge gave a contented squeak.

"Oh, yes," Lewis answered, not really looking at Marge at all.

"Okay," Denman said, wading to the edge of the pool and leaving Marge to frolic playfully in the pool. "Can you take this for me?" She handed Lewis an underwater camera that she'd been using.

"Yes, I can." Lewis answered confidently.

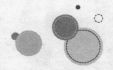

He took the camera from her and placed it carefully on the timber ramp that led back up to the lab.

When he turned back Denman was still standing knee-deep in the pool, struggling to get her arms out of her wetsuit.

"Uh, can you give me a hand with this?" she asked, looking at him with a grin.

"Yes … I can. Yes. I can do that," Lewis stammered awkwardly.

He stood behind her and, grabbing the shoulders of the wetsuit, peeled it down, like he was peeling a banana.

Lewis gulped, trying desperately to retain an air of professionalism and *not* look at the bikini Denman was wearing beneath her wetsuit.

"Thank you," she said, wriggling her arms free and shaking the excess water off them.

"Okay," Denman said, all business, "now

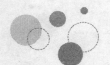

let me show you where you'll be working," She hopped out of the pool and grabbed a towel to quickly dry off her hair before leading Lewis back up towards the lab. He followed eagerly.

Once they were inside, Denman disappeared behind one of the doors leading off from the lab while she went and changed back into her normal clothes. Not knowing what else to do with himself, Lewis decided to ask her how she became interested in science.

"So how did you end up here?" he called out.

"In this lab, or in science generally?" she yelled back through the door.

"In science," he answered. "How does a woman like you get to be one of the world's leading experts in mammalian evolution?"

"Well, I guess it all began when I was a kid," Denman answered, her voice a bit muffled through the door. "Even when I was young I loved the ocean. I remember we used to go

on holidays to the beach when I was little. My brothers were into surfing, but I'd just spend every day walking along the beach exploring the rock-pools and collecting things. Whenever we went back home at the end of the holiday, my dad would have to make extra room in the car for all the jars and containers I'd used to collect starfish and jellyfish and shells and things. And then I'd sit in my room for hours studying them. Sometimes I'd cut them up to see if I could figure out how they worked, but mostly I'd just draw pictures of them and see how long I could keep them alive."

"So did you know you wanted to be a marine biologist back then?" Lewis asked her as he wandered around the lab.

"I don't think so," Denman called back. "It wasn't until early in high school when I had a biology teacher that taught me all about the value of science. She was the one that got me interested in reading Charles Darwin."

"*On the Origin of Species*?" Lewis asked.

"Of course," Denman answered. "Even though I knew a bit about evolution, it wasn't until I started to read all about what Darwin actually did that I realized I wanted to try and develop his ideas further."

"And then you went to uni?" Lewis asked.

"Yep. Then I went to uni, started working towards my PhD and ended up being chosen to represent the university on an international team studying aquatic ecology at the Charles Darwin Research Station on Santa Cruz in the Galapagos Islands. In the end, the project lost its funding but I didn't want to leave. I still felt like I had so much to discover out there ..."

Suddenly, Denman stepped back into the lab, tying her hair back with an elastic band. Lewis was grateful to see that she was fully clothed, right down to a conservative-looking white lab-coat. At least that was one less distraction he'd have to deal with.

"... so, my work in the Galapagos Islands took a bit of a left turn and that's how I ended up studying cell mutation in mammals," she finished. "Who knew it would generate so much interest in the scientific community."

"Incredible," Lewis mumbled, still gazing around at all the equipment in the lab.

"I beg your pardon?" Denman asked.

"Huh?" Lewis answered vaguely, his attention focused on a beaker he was holding up to examine. "Oh, er, it's just this equipment. I've read about it, but it's just ... wow," he said, placing the beaker carefully back on the bench.

"Yep, well this is what you get when people throw money at your next research project." Denman explained.

"It's fantastic," Lewis said, itching to get his hands on the centrifuge he was standing next to.

"So which piece am I on?" he asked enthusiastically. "The electron microscope?"

He trotted over to the bench that held the electron microscope. "No," he said, suddenly spotting an even bigger piece of apparatus. "The ion evaporator?" He raced up to it but got distracted on the way by something even more impressive. "The atomic absorption photometer," he said finally, standing proudly beside it.

"How about we start with the mop?" Denman suggested, holding a mop out towards him.

"Oh," Lewis answered disappointedly.

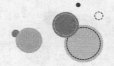

Chapter 6

Standing opposite Lewis in Emma's kitchen, Cleo was horrified.

"You mopped floors?" she asked disbelievingly. *There I was thinking he was off making some great scientific sacrifice for us and she's got him mopping floors! I don't know what's worse, Lewis having a crush on her or the fact that he'll mop floors for her. I bet he wouldn't mop the floor for me*, she thought, pouting slightly in Lewis's direction.

"And that helps us *how* exactly?" Rikki asked as she pulled a pizza box from the oven. It was last night's pizza, but Rikki had no qualms about heating it up and eating it – she was hungry! Emma gave her a disapproving look, as if to say, *you're not actually thinking of eating that are you?* Rikki opened up the box and took out the largest slice she could find.

She took a big bite and let the topping drip down her chin, giving Emma a big cheesy grin.

"Guys, I know what I'm doing," Lewis said defensively. "I have access to her lab. All I need now is a fresh DNA sample, say … a toenail clipping?" he suggested, reaching behind him and pulling out a pair of nail clippers.

Rikki almost choked on her pizza at the suggestion. Eating day-old pizza was one thing, but handing over a toenail clipping? Even she had her standards.

Emma just turned up her nose. There was no way anyone was getting their hands on one of *her* toenail clippings. *Even I don't like touching them once they're off my toes,* she thought. *Yuck!* She looked at Cleo expectantly.

Surprisingly, Cleo had absolutely no problem with Lewis's suggestion at all. Toenails were just toenails as far as she was concerned. Thinking about it a bit more, she realized she didn't necessarily like the idea of being the one

that was being experimented on. But this *was* in the name of science after all.

"Okay, okay," said Cleo, grabbing the clippers from Lewis and heading off to the bathroom. *No one said I have to clip them off in front of everyone!*

The next morning, Lewis got up early. He wanted to make it to the lab before Dr Denman arrived, so he skipped breakfast, grabbed his backpack and Cleo's toenail clipping and raced straight out of the house.

He knew exactly what he had to do; he just hoped that the lab would be empty when he got there. If it was, then he was fairly certain he'd be able to get everything done and cleaned up before Denman arrived. With luck, she wouldn't even know he'd been there.

By the time he arrived at the marine park, Lewis had everything already planned out in his head. He knew the layout of the

laboratory and knew exactly where each piece of equipment he would need was located. He even had everything timed out using songs – he'd seen that in a movie once, where a team of professional jewel-thieves timed each step of their heists using songs. If they knew it took three minutes and 42 seconds before the security guards responded to an alarm, then they'd sing a song that ran for exactly three minutes and 42 seconds. That way they knew exactly how much time they had up their sleeves.

Standing at the lab door, Lewis took a deep breath before swiping his access card. Now that Denman had given him the research assistant's job, he had no need for Cleo's card. He walked in.

To Lewis's great disappointment, Dr Denman stood working at one of the benches. She turned to smile at him, but Lewis' heart sank. *Great,* he thought, *all that planning for nothing.* Now he had to come up with an excuse

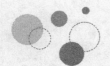
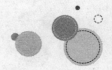

for being there so early in the morning. Quickly weighing up his options and deciding that it would look too weird just walking out again, he decided that he'd just have to try to make the best of a bad situation and wing it.

"Ah, I just missed a couple of bench tops," he blurted out quickly as he closed the door behind him. "I thought I'd come back and get them done."

"Very thorough," Denman said, nodding her head approvingly as she looked Lewis up and down. "Okay, well I'm just about to pop out."

"Oh, yeah, well don't let me stop you," Lewis said, his hopes soaring again. *Perhaps I will get some time alone here after all*, he thought. "I'm sure I can handle a few old bench tops," he said out loud.

"Okay, I'll leave you to it," Denman said as she headed out of the door.

Perfect! thought Lewis. *Now's my only chance. I just hope she's gone long enough to*

get some work done. He raced to the door and listened closely until the sound of Denman's heels walking down the ramp outside had faded, then got straight to work.

He turned and ran back across the laboratory, sliding on the lino floor and stopping right in front of the optical microscope. Pulling the phial containing Cleo's toenail clipping from his bag, he grabbed a scalpel from the bench top and sliced off a small sample from the edge of the nail, mounting it carefully onto a glass slide and then hurriedly placing the slide under the microscope. He had to see if he could spot anything unique about the cells. Perhaps there was something particular about the cell-wall structure that would give him a clue about why the girls had such a drastic reaction to water.

Lewis focused the microscope and pulled up a larger display on the computer screen beside him. He studied it for a moment before picking up a pipette from a nearby rack and

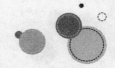

filling it with a saline solution. *Perhaps if I can see the reaction to water at the cellular level*, he wondered.

"Having fun?" Denman's voice asked suddenly from behind him.

Lewis looked up. He'd been sprung!

"Oh, um, I was just …" Lewis stammered, racking his brain for an excuse that would save him.

"Hey, relax," Denman smiled. "I knew you couldn't resist," she added, as if she would have done exactly the same thing in his position. "Bench tops? Puh-lease."

Lewis smiled nervously. *She thinks I'm just using the equipment for fun*, he thought. *If I can just keep her thinking that, then maybe this isn't a lost cause after all.*

Thankfully, when Lewis had looked up and seen Denman standing there, he'd jumped backwards and accidentally knocked the keyboard beside him, hitting the display toggle

and switching the computer screen off in the process; at least she wouldn't be able to see anything from across the room. He just had to stop her from getting close enough to the microscope that she'd be tempted to take a look at what he'd been studying.

"So, what are you looking at?" Denman asked, closing the door behind her. It was precisely the question Lewis hadn't wanted her to ask.

"Oh, nothing," Lewis answered lightly. "Just something … that I found at the beach." Lame as it was, it was the only thing that came into his head that seemed even remotely plausible. "It's sand or something, it's nothing special."

"There's no such thing as nothing special," Denman said, walking towards the bench and eyeing the microscope with curiosity. "Everything has its own story to tell."

Lewis began to panic. *If she takes one more step*, he thought, *she's going to see a whole lot*

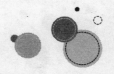

more than sand. And I'm going to have a whole lot more explaining to do. He had to think fast.

"Oooh, is that the time?" he asked suddenly, pretending to look at his watch as he said it but actually looking down at the bench top to gauge how close the phial containing Cleo's toenail sample was to his hand. *If I can just grab it quickly enough.*

"I've gotta get to school," Lewis blurted out abruptly. Then without waiting another second, he grabbed the phial, swung his backpack up off the floor and over his shoulder, and headed straight for the door all in one fluid movement. He brushed past Denman as he left, almost bumping into her, but kept on going without looking back. Lewis didn't care how rude Denman thought his behaviour was – he could deal with that later – all that mattered was that he was out of there, with Cleo's toenail sample clasped safely in his hand.

As soon as he was out of the lab with the door closed behind him, Lewis leaned against

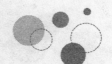

the wall for a moment to catch his breath. He had done it – just! *But that was too close for comfort*, he thought.

What Lewis didn't realize, however, was that on the other side of the laboratory wall Denman was heading straight for the microscope. Just as he was outside thinking how close his escape had been, she was inside flicking the display screen back up on the computer and gazing at the screen.

"What have we here?" she said to herself quietly, peering through the eyepiece to get a closer look at whatever it was that Lewis had been so interested in.

The cells were obviously human, but not like any human cells she'd seen before. Intrigued, Denman picked up the pipette that Lewis had left lying beside the microscope and carefully dropped some saline onto the slide.

To her complete amazement, within seconds of coming into contact with the salt water the

cells seemed to become suddenly agitated, bouncing about on the monitor as if they were somehow energized by the water. Just when she thought things couldn't get any stranger, the cells began to change their structure entirely, bursting into irregular shapes and patterns that looked almost like crystals. It was as if they were mutating before her eyes.

If Lewis had still been in the room, he would have seen her take a sudden step back from the microscope, silently mouthing the words 'oh my gosh' before stumbling onto the stool beside her in shock.

But instead, Lewis was making his way back along the path that ran beside the dolphin pool. He was still a little shaken up by how close he'd come to being found out, but he thought he'd got away with it.

She must think I'm a complete idiot, he thought, wondering what Denman would say the next time she saw him. *But it's probably better than Cleo thinking the same thing. Okay,*

now, I've got everything. The phial is in my pocket. He checked his back pocket. *Check. Cleo's toenail is in the phial. Check. The slide is in my ... in my ...* Lewis checked all his pockets again. It wasn't there. *The slide is in my ...* He checked his backpack. Suddenly, Lewis remembered exactly where the slide was and his heart sank to the pit of his stomach. In his desperation to get the phial safely out of Denman's sight, he'd forgotten all about the slide that was still mounted under the microscope. *Oh no!!!* thought Lewis, realizing what he'd done. *No, no, no!*

Without wasting another moment, he raced back up the path, up the ramp and swung open the door to the laboratory.

To his amazement, when he barged in through the door, Dr Denman was sitting at one of the benches making an entry in her notepad. She wasn't even sitting near the microscope. *Maybe she hasn't even looked at it,* Lewis thought hopefully.

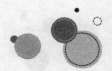

"Dr Denman, I think I left my–" he began to say.

"Your slide?" Denman interrupted him, handing him a slide box. "Hmm, I know it's not sand, Lewis. In fact, I'm not sure what it is."

Lewis took the box from her, his hand trembling slightly as he realized what she was saying. She'd seen the sample. He felt like a fool for thinking that she might not have looked at it.

"It's … it's a private project," he explained, half hoping that she wouldn't ask any more questions but realizing deep down how hopeless the situation was. *She's not going to buy that*, he thought. *If she's any kind of scientist at all, she'll want to know exactly what she was looking at, and I'm completely out of excuses.* Standing there holding the slide, Lewis just couldn't see how he was going to get out of there with the girls' secret still safe.

"Okay." Denman said, smiling as if it really was okay. "That's fine."

Lewis was stunned. *Fine? Where are you seeing anything that's fine about this? You've just seen* mermaid *cells and you're saying that everything's fine?* He kept his mouth shut.

"So listen," Denman continued. "Um, I'm doing another dive tomorrow and I need some assistance. Feel like doing some work experience?"

"Oh, yeah," Lewis answered, starting to relax slightly. *She's actually going to leave it at that,* he thought hopefully. He looked at her for a moment, weighing up the possibility that this was all just part of some elaborate plan to fool him into telling her where the sample had come from. But Denman just smiled back at him innocently, as if the sample was the furthest thing from her mind. *Maybe she* can *be trusted,* he thought. *And after all, who am I to say no to a beautiful, trustworthy scientist asking me to come on a dive with her? Besides, perhaps by going on a dive with her, I can find out a bit more about the kind of procedures she might use*

to investigate the properties of a DNA sample.

"That sounds cool," he answered enthusiastically.

"I'll see you then?" Denman asked, tapping her pen on her notebook as if she was keen to get back to her work.

"Okay, yeah," Lewis answered, walking back out the door with the slide box safely in his hand.

Lewis couldn't have been more relieved. He had the slide back. He had the rest of Cleo's toenail sample in his pocket and he was going on a dive tomorrow with Dr Denman. Things couldn't have turned out better.

As soon as the door had closed, Denman looked back to the bench top and opened up another box that had been sitting there. Inside the box was Lewis's slide, complete with Cleo's toenail.

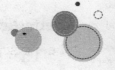

Chapter 7

"Lewis, she saw the sample! How *could* you?" Emma scowled. She was sitting on the edge of Cleo's bed, with Cleo and Rikki beside her, all of them facing Lewis accusingly. He was standing in front of Cleo's dressing table and had just finished telling them what had happened that afternoon at Denman's lab. From the look on his face, Emma thought he was actually happy about how it had all turned out! *Can't he see what he's done*, she thought. *I knew we should never have trusted him with something so important! Now she's going to run off to the first university that'll listen to her and before we know it, the whole world will know we're mermaids!*

"You're not getting the big picture!" Lewis argued, slumping into the only chair in Cleo's room. "It was an *accident*. And besides," he

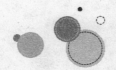

added, leaning towards them meaningfully, "she's a scientist. This is what scientists do."

"What, sell out their friends?" Rikki scoffed heatedly. Right from the start, she'd thought this whole Dr Denman plan had been a bad idea and as much as she tried not to say 'I told you so', she was finding it increasingly difficult to keep the words from her lips. She had seen enough films about evil scientists to know that they weren't exactly the most trustworthy bunch of people around. Sure, maybe there were a few of them out there trying to do some good in the world – they didn't give away Nobel prizes for nothing – but Rikki knew that history was riddled with more than enough stories of power-hungry scientists. And from those stories, she had the distinct impression that selling out their friends was precisely what some scientists seemed to excel at. She almost felt like asking Lewis whether the name Dr Frankenstein rang any bells.

"No," Lewis answered, exasperated.

"Compare notes. That's the thing about us."

"Us?" Rikki said, with a look of disgust. The last thing she wanted was to be lumped in with someone like Dr Denman.

"No, we *scientists*," Lewis explained, trying to keep the frustration he felt out of his voice. "Our need to know is what drives us. Believe me, she's cool."

"What if her 'need to know' ends up with her dissecting us?" Rikki asked, looking to Emma and Cleo for support. They both nodded emphatically. None of them wanted to end up as sushi on some stainless-steel table in a laboratory, with men and women in white coats prodding them as they tried to figure out exactly how a mermaid's tail worked.

"She's not *like* that," Lewis answered. As far as he was concerned, the conversation was going nowhere. *Great!* he thought sarcastically. *Now we're back at the dissection table! If only they could have seen what I saw at the lab, then*

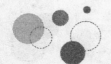

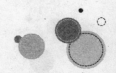

they'd understand. Dr Denman's not like other people. She's the kind of scientist that I want to be – not some power-hungry busy-body wanting to get her hands on every piece of information she can. But they don't seem to want to understand that, no matter how I explain it.

"I have to go," he said eventually, getting up from the chair with a sigh and walking towards Cleo's door. "I'll talk to you tomorrow," he added wearily, closing the door behind him as he left.

"Lewis isn't usually this erratic," Cleo said, turning to Emma and Rikki as soon as Lewis was gone.

They both looked at her doubtfully. They had all seen how Lewis had been on the phone to Denman at the Juice-Net Café and there was nothing that would convince them that he wasn't completely smitten with her. Lewis might have been trustworthy under normal circumstances, but these were *not* normal circumstances. Whatever was going on between

him and Denman, it had changed Lewis, and that meant they were going to have to watch their backs for a while.

"Those in favour of not trusting Lewis as far as we could throw him, raise your hands," Rikki said, throwing both of her hands in the air emphatically.

"Agreed," Emma said, raising her hand a bit more reluctantly than Rikki. "Let's keep an eye on him."

Cleo sighed. As much as she hated to admit it, she knew that Rikki and Emma were probably right. They *did* need to keep an eye on Lewis for a while. *I can't believe I'm going to go behind Lewis's back*, she thought regretfully. *I never thought I'd do anything like this.* Cleo suddenly felt like she needed a drink of water, or at least something that would get rid of the bad taste in her mouth.

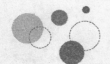

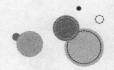

Chapter 8

Cleo still felt awful about spying on Lewis, even if Emma and Rikki *were* right. But she had to admit, it was a little bit exciting, sneaking around like undercover agents. Before they'd left her house that morning, she'd tried to convince Emma and Rikki that they should all be dressed from head to toe in black, like real spies. But Emma had just rolled her eyes and said she was taking things too far. As far as Cleo was concerned, though, it never hurt to be dressed for the occasion. Even now, as the three of them crouched behind some old packing crates watching Denman and Lewis load up their boat with boxes of equipment from the pier, Cleo still thought she'd feel a lot more comfortable in a pair of black tights and a black roll-necked jersey.

Thankfully, when they'd arrived at the

pier, Denman and Lewis had been deep in conversation and hadn't once taken their eyes off each other, so Cleo was certain they hadn't been seen. *Actually*, she thought, *the way Lewis is hanging on every word Denman says, we could have turned into mermaids over here and he still wouldn't have noticed us!* Suddenly, Cleo felt a sharp nudge in her ribs and turned to see Rikki glaring at her.

"Shhhh!" Rikki whispered.

"What?" Cleo asked innocently. She hadn't even realized that she'd been laughing to herself at the thought of them all lying on the pier with their tails flapping against the decking. Still smiling, she crouched down lower behind her crate and listened closely to what Denman and Lewis were saying to each other.

"Science isn't just about satisfying your own curiosity, Lewis," she heard Denman say. "It has to have a purpose. It has to be better for everyone."

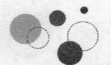

Do all scientists spend their time lecturing people? Cleo wondered.

"Oh, yeah, I'm so totally there," Lewis replied as if he was actually enjoying the lecture. "Only science can change the world, Dr Denman."

Cleo rolled her eyes towards Emma and Rikki.

"What a suck," Rikki whispered to her.

"Lewis, please," Denman went on. "If we're going to be working together, call me Linda."

"Linda?" Lewis asked, sounding shocked and disappointed at the same time. "Why?"

Cleo thought he almost sounded as if he preferred calling her Dr Denman. *That'd be just like Lewis*, she thought. *He does tend to be overly impressed by titles, particularly academic titles.* She snickered to herself, imagining how Lewis would act if he ever met a professor – it'd almost be too much for him to cope with! Beside her, Rikki scoffed quietly as if she was

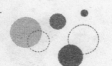

thinking exactly the same thing.

"It's my name," Denman answered simply.

"Oh," Lewis said, still sounding a bit disappointed. "So," he said more cheerily as he hoisted another box over to Denman's side of the boat, "Do we need all this stuff?"

"Yep, we'll use most of this stuff today," Denman answered. "That's the other thing about science, Lewis," she explained as she took an underwater camera from him and placed it with the other equipment they'd been stacking neatly on the deck. "All the toys are a hoot."

"So, where are we heading?" Lewis asked casually.

"I was thinking Mako Island," Denman answered, causing Lewis to almost drop the scuba gear he was about to pass to her.

"Mako Island?" he shrieked, before quickly steadying his voice. "Ah, that's not a good idea. There's nothing to see."

Cleo almost shrieked herself, but another sharp jab to the ribs from Rikki quickly silenced her. They couldn't afford to blow their cover now. They just had to wait and see how things panned out. *But Mako Island?* thought Cleo. *Lewis can't take her there – he knows that. Surely he can't be that infatuated with her that he'd consider taking her to Mako Island. Come on Lewis! Talk your way out of this!*

Cleo looked back towards the boat to see Denman staring at Lewis questioningly. Again, Lewis was just standing there doing that thing where he moved his mouth, but didn't make any sound.

"No, nothing to see at all,' Lewis eventually spluttered out, managing to keep at least some of the anxiety from his voice. "And it's full of sharks," he went on more confidently. "Lots of big …"

"Come on, Lewis, don't tell me you're *afraid* of sharks?" Denman teased.

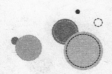

"Me? No, not at all," Lewis answered, suddenly realizing that he was cornered. He couldn't let Denman think he was afraid of sharks. And he couldn't let her go to Mako Island. But he also appreciated that aside from telling her the real reason, he couldn't think of even a half-reasonable excuse why they shouldn't go. With a sigh, he realized he was completely stuck. "Mako Island's fine," he mumbled.

"Good," Denman said with an air of finality. They were heading to Mako Island whether Lewis liked it or not. With a look of resignation, Lewis picked up the last of the diving equipment from the pier and heaved it over to the boat's deck, before leaping onto the boat himself.

Cleo turned immediately to Rikki and Emma as the boat's engines roared into life. They both looked just as worried as her.

"He's nuts," Rikki said. "He's *completely* nuts. How can he take her there?"

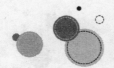

"We've got to get there before them,"
Emma said decisively. Rikki and Cleo nodded
their heads in agreement. They had to get to
Mako Island before Denman's boat did. Even
if Lewis and Denman didn't end up diving
anywhere near the moon-pool, the whole area
around Mako Island was risky territory and the
safest option was to keep a close eye on them.

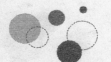

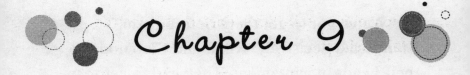

Chapter 9

Without saying another word, Cleo, Rikki and Emma raced around to the other side of the marina as soon as Denman's boat was out of sight. After quickly glancing around to check that no one could see them, they dived into the water. Denman and Lewis already had a head start and they couldn't afford to waste a single second. They had to get to Mako Island before the boat did.

Within moments of hitting the water's surface, the three girls felt the familiar tingling sensation of their mermaid transformations – the warm shiver from the tips of their fingers to the ends of the toes, until their legs were replaced entirely by their powerful tails. Deep beneath the water, they gave each other a quick, knowing smile and then, with almost

 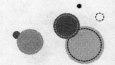

synchronized tail-flicks, darted off towards
Mako Island.

As they raced along, Cleo gave a small,
bubbly sigh of relief when she saw Denman's
boat off to their left-hand side – they had
caught up with it and would be at Mako Island
before Lewis and Dr Denman arrived. She
motioned to Emma and Rikki and they each
gave her a brief, comprehending nod. They had
seen the boat too. But that didn't mean they
could relax just yet; they still wanted to be in
position when Denman and Lewis arrived. So
they powered on through the water, slowing
only when they caught sight of the reef that
encircled the island and then sinking down to
the ocean floor amongst the rocks and kelp,
they waited silently for the boat to arrive.

They didn't have to wait long.

Within minutes, they saw the boat's
propellers churning a frothy path towards
them. They sat on the ocean floor as the boat

steered to a spot almost directly above them, then drifted silently as the engines were cut. It floated for a few more metres and then came to a jolting halt as the anchor sank down through the water and hooked itself on to the edge of the reef. Cleo sat nervously watching the boat bobbing rhythmically up and down. From her position behind a large, coral-encrusted rock that jutted out from the reef, she could just make out the two shapes of Lewis and Dr Denman sitting on the boat's side railing. She saw Lewis adjust the scuba tank that was strapped to his back before lowering his mask over his eyes and giving Denman two thumbs up. Then the two of them flipped backwards off the railing and plunged head first into the sea.

Cleo watched as Denman and Lewis dived down to the reef. With the sunlight behind them, they looked like two black sea lions twisting their way down through the depths. Bright shards of light pierced the water all around them. At any other time, Cleo would

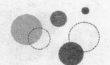

have thought it was a beautiful sight, but right now, she was scared. Denman and Lewis were diving straight towards the underwater cave entrance to the moon-pool! She felt Emma squeeze her hand tightly. *If Denman finds her way to that cave*, Cleo thought, *we might as well say goodbye to any hope of not ending up on the dissection table.*

Even though she didn't have to, Cleo held her breath. Denman was almost at the cave. Cleo knew that the cave entrance was partly hidden behind a large swathe of seaweed, but even so, she had no doubt that if Denman gave just a few more kicks of her flippers, she'd pretty much stumble across the cave without even looking for it. And once she saw it, nothing would keep her from going in for a closer look.

But then Denman suddenly swam in completely the opposite direction! *Where's she going?* Cleo thought delightedly, wondering what could have possibly caused anyone to

suddenly veer off like that. And then she spotted Lewis. He had positioned himself close to a beautiful cluster of mushroom coral and was gesturing for Denman to come over and help him take some samples. He had saved them!

Cleo was sure Lewis hadn't known what he was doing – after all, Lewis had never even *seen* the underwater entrance to the cave – but whether he knew what he was doing or not, Lewis had just helped them avoid a major catastrophe. Cleo could have swum over and given him an underwater hug there and then she was so happy. But her happiness was gradually replaced by another emotion entirely. As her heartbeat slowed and she began to realize they were out of immediate danger, she started to realize how annoyed she was with Lewis. *Whether he's saved us or not, how could he be so irresponsible?* she thought. *We wouldn't even be in this situation if it wasn't for Lewis! If he hadn't been so keen to go diving*

with her, we'd never have needed to chase that boat and I wouldn't be sitting here on the ocean floor squeezing Emma's hand and worrying about whether or not Denman was going to stumble across the entrance to the moon-pool. This is all Lewis's fault! she thought irritably. *Lewis and his newfound weakness for blondes!*

When Lewis and Denman arrived back at the marina, Lewis didn't even hang around to help unload any of their diving equipment. As soon as the boat was safely moored, he jumped from the deck onto the jetty, yelled out to Denman that he'd just remembered he was late for an appointment, and took off towards Emma's house. Denman might not have seen anything suspicious beneath the water, but Lewis certainly had and it definitely wasn't a dolphin's tail that had caught his eye.

By the time he reached Emma's front door, he'd worked himself up into quite a state. *How could they?* he thought. *One minute they're*

accusing me *of not being careful enough and the next, they're swimming around in front of her, almost parading their mermaid tails for the whole world to see. What were they thinking?* What really had him worked up was the fact that the girls clearly didn't trust him at all. *What are they thinking, spying on me like that?* He just couldn't understand what he'd done to deserve being spied on – it was such a betrayal after all the effort he'd made to protect their secret.

"You think I wouldn't notice you guys spying on me?" he said to Emma as soon as she opened the front door. Cleo and Rikki were standing right behind her. "I mean, where's the trust?" he added, looking each of them in the eye.

"The trust?" Emma replied, closing the door and walking back towards the kitchen. "I think it died when you *accidentally* gave our DNA to a world-renowned marine biologist."

"No," Rikki said bitterly. "No, I *think* it was

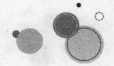

when he agreed to take Dr Baywatch Babe on a date to Mako Island."

"You've gone too far, Lewis," Cleo added, turning to face him.

This is ridiculous, thought Lewis. *They really believe that I would betray their trust. After everything I've done for them. I guess it's not really that surprising coming from Rikki, or even from Emma, but from Cleo? This is just one step too far. I really thought she knew me better than that, but I guess I was wrong.*

"You don't trust me?" he said aloud, the tone of his voice letting them know just how hurt he was by their accusations. "After everything we've been through?"

Emma and Rikki just stared back at him blankly, as if to say that as far as they were concerned, 'they' actually hadn't been through anything together. Unable to meet Lewis's gaze, Cleo looked away miserably. She knew that Lewis had been a big part of everything

they'd been through since that first night on Mako Island, and up until a few days ago, she'd been grateful beyond words that she'd been able to share everything with him. But now that Denman was part of the equation, she knew deep down that all of that was about to change. The thought almost made her want to cry.

"I have been working *so* hard," Lewis explained, his voice cracking slightly. "Trying to solve basic questions about … about why you guys are the way you are … and this is what it comes down to?"

"They're *our* lives Lewis," Rikki replied angrily, taking a seat between Emma and Cleo at the kitchen table so that all three of them faced him. "*We're* being careful. Maybe *you* should be too."

Lewis looked shocked and hurt. *All this time I thought we were in this together,* he thought. *But obviously they just think this is all about them. If that's the case, why did they even ask for my help at all? If they want to deal with*

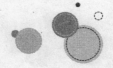

this themselves, then maybe they should. Forget about the fact that science is the only thing that can possibly give them the answers they're looking for. As far as I'm concerned, they're on their own.

"Do you wanna know what *I* think?" he said, his mind already made up that he was going to tell them exactly what he thought whether they liked it or not. "I think you guys are a bunch of kids."

Rikki looked stunned, as if she never expected to hear something like that from Lewis. And if Rikki looked stunned, Emma and Cleo looked utterly horrified. They didn't just think they'd never hear anything like this from Lewis; up until that second, they would have said it just wasn't possible for Lewis to say anything so venomous.

"*And*," Lewis added, looking at each of them in turn. "At least Dr Denman is a woman ... and a little bit more ... mature."

Without saying another word, Lewis turned and stormed out of the kitchen, leaving Emma and Rikki sitting there open-mouthed and Cleo staring blankly after him in shock. None of them even moved until they heard the splintering crack of the front door as Lewis slammed it shut behind him. Cleo was glad he was gone. She was glad he wasn't around to see her tears.

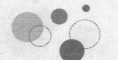

Chapter 10

It wasn't until Lewis reached the marine park gate that he began to calm down again. In fact, when he got there, he couldn't even remember the walk over from Emma's house, he was so angry. All he knew was that he'd practically stomped the whole way there – and the main reason he knew that was because of the dull ache in his heels. *I should really wear better shoes if I'm going to be doing a lot of angry stomping,* he thought, trying to see the lighter side of things. But he felt so let down by Cleo, Emma and Rikki. Well, more let down by Cleo than anyone else.

Of all the people in the world, he thought. *I always thought she'd be the one to trust me to do the right thing by her. Cleo should know that I've always had her best interests at heart. Sure, I might get a bit carried away by the excitement*

of science from time to time, but I'd never betray her and she should know that.

Suddenly looking up, Lewis realized that he was standing in front of the door to Denman's lab. He shook his head, trying to clear his thoughts, and then gave a few quick knocks on the door before walking straight in.

Denman was sitting at the bench at the far end of the lab, furthest from the door. Lewis saw her quickly close her laptop as he shut the door behind him, but didn't think anything of it.

"Lewis!" Denman called out to him cheerily, turning around in her chair to face him.

"Hello," he answered as brightly as he could, which wasn't very brightly at all given how miserable he was feeling.

"Back again?" Denman asked, raising her eyebrows slightly as if she was surprised to see him again so soon. "You've really got to get a life."

"What about you?" Lewis answered, picking

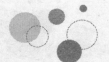
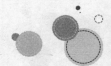

up a flask containing a preserved starfish and holding it up for a closer look. "You're always here."

"This *is* my life," Denman replied with a smile.

"Yeah, well one day I hope it's mine too," Lewis said, putting the flask back on the shelf and pulling up a chair opposite her.

"Maybe sooner than you think," she said mysteriously.

"Wha–?" Lewis started to ask.

"Lewis," Denman said, putting down her notepad and looking at Lewis with a very serious expression, as if she wanted to tell him something of critical importance. "I've just received a very large research grant from a corporation to do a six-month scientific survey on an area of my choice."

"Really?" Lewis asked, genuinely happy to hear such news. He knew what a rare opportunity this was within the scientific

community, so he had a fair idea of how thrilled Denman must have been. "Oh wow, congratulations. You really–"

"I want you on my team," Denman interrupted him suddenly. "You and me, Lewis. It'll mean full-time work; a lot of travel, even international travel." She paused for a moment to take in Lewis's reaction. " What do you think?"

"Wh-wh-wh …" Lewis stuttered. He didn't know what he thought. He definitely didn't know what to say. *A six-month research project*! This was exactly the kind of work he'd always dreamed of doing and now that the opportunity was sitting right in front of him for the taking, he didn't know how to react. Six months! Away from home, away from school, away from Cleo … "Er …" he stammered.

"I've already contacted your teachers," Denman went on, sensing that Lewis wasn't quite sure what to say. "There's government

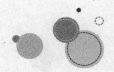

funding available to subsidize your trip and you'll even get credit for the work."

"I dunno," Lewis started to say, realizing that Denman had thought of everything. "I'll have to–"

"Ask your parents, of course," Denman interrupted again, looking both hopeful that he'd say yes and understanding that he'd need some time to talk it over with his family and friends. "But I'll need you to make a decision tomorrow."

Lewis was stunned. Everything he'd always wanted was suddenly within his reach and all he had to do was say yes. He knew he had to think quickly – opportunities like this just didn't come along every day, but he also didn't want to rush into anything without thinking it all through. A decision like this could have far-reaching consequences, both good and bad, and Lewis wanted to be fully aware of the bad ones before making his decision.

"I'll be leaving for my lab in the Galapagos Islands the day after," Denman added, complicating things even further. "That's where we'll be based."

"Wow," Lewis said, leaning back in his chair and clasping his hands together behind his neck. He was already dreaming of what his life would be like if he said yes to Denman. *The Galapagos Islands! Me in the Galapagos Islands!! Me with Dr Denman in the Galapagos Islands!!! And all the research equipment we'll ever need. This is just too incredible to be true. But things that seem too good to be true usually* are *too good to be true. I really need to think about this.*

Rousing himself back to reality, Lewis looked across the bench top to see Denman still looking at him expectantly.

"Right, well, I'll have a think about it and let you know tomorrow," he said, pushing back his chair and making his way back towards the door. He realized he was a little unsteady on his feet; it was all such a huge shock. Grabbing

the door handle for balance, he turned back to Denman and smiled. "You need my answer tomorrow?" he asked, just to be sure he'd heard her correctly.

"Tomorrow," she confirmed with a smile.

Regardless of the tension that had flared up between them after the dive off Mako Island, faced with such a life-changing decision, the first thing Lewis wanted to do was talk it over with Cleo. She might not have been his favourite person at that particular point in time, but she was still his best friend and he valued her opinion just as much as ever.

As soon as he left Denman's office, he called Cleo's mobile and asked her to meet him in the park next to the marina. She'd sounded hesitant at first, but as soon as he said that he needed her advice about a big decision he had to make, she'd said she would be there as soon as she could.

And true to her word, she was there at the park waiting when Lewis arrived.

"Wow! That's amazing, isn't it?" Cleo asked as soon as Lewis had finished telling her about Denman's offer. She was sitting beside him on the edge of the pier, their legs dangling over the side as they both leaned back to soak up the last rays of the slowly setting sun.

"Well, it's certainly a once-in-a-lifetime opportunity, yeah," Lewis answered distractedly as he stared out to sea. He was still definitely a long way from making up his mind one way or the other, and although he was listening carefully to every word of advice Cleo gave him, he was also deep in thought. His mind raced with the possibilities of it all. *Just think, the day after tomorrow I could be on a boat heading for the Galapagos Islands!* he thought. *In two days' time!*

"What are you going to do?" Cleo asked, folding her legs back under her and turning towards Lewis. He shook himself out of his

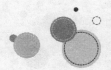

stare and turned slightly towards her.

"I dunno," he answered less vaguely. "I'm just so happy that she thinks I'm smart enough to do it."

"Oh please," Cleo said, as if she thought the real reason Denman had asked him to join her on the project had nothing to do with how smart she thought he was.

"What?" asked Lewis, wondering what Cleo was getting at.

"You really think she wants you for your brain?" Cleo asked.

"It's not like that between Dr Denman and I at all," Lewis answered, somewhat defensively. *Does Cleo think there's some kind of romance going on between Denman and I?* Lewis thought suddenly. *But that's ridiculous! Although … I guess it would explain why the three of them think I would betray them – if they think I'm in love with Denman then perhaps they think I'd do pretty much anything for her.*

"That's *not* what I mean," Cleo explained. "I mean, how do you know she's not just after another sample?"

Right, thought Lewis. *So that's it. She doesn't think this is about Denman and I at all. She still thinks it's all about her.*

"No," he said aloud. "No, she's forgotten all about that." *Why couldn't Cleo think for once that this wasn't about her and her mermaidness? Is the idea that someone might actually think I'm talented enough to undertake this kind of research really that far-fetched?* He was starting to regret asking for Cleo's advice, but decided to give it one last shot.

"So, what do you think I should do?" he asked.

"Well, like you said, it's a once-in-a-lifetime opportunity," Cleo said, trying to think of what she would do if she were faced with a similar choice. "And it's what you've always wanted."

She was trying to be as objective as she

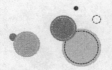

could, weighing up the pros and cons in the same way she thought Lewis would if their situations were reversed. But no matter how objective she tried to be, all she could think of was what her life would be like without Lewis. No Lewis to talk to when she needed some advice of her own. No Lewis making her laugh when she needed cheering up. And no Lewis to share her secrets with. She didn't want to tell him she thought he should stay just because she wanted him to, but at the same time, the more she thought about it, the more she began to realize just how important Lewis was to her, and that fact alone was clouding her judgement and stopping her from thinking straight.

And there was something else too. Something beyond her friendship with Lewis and how much she liked having him around. Something completely irrational and crazy; it was almost as if she was … *into* Lewis! *But that's ridiculous*, thought Cleo. *I'm not into Lewis. I just like him as a friend.* Try as she

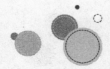

might to be rational though, in her head it all came down to the fact that she wanted Lewis to stay.

"And there's nothing holding you here ... *right*?" she asked hopefully, looking at him searchingly. *Maybe he's thinking the same thing as I am*, she thought. *Maybe he wants to go, but realizes that he couldn't stand to be away from me? Or at least, maybe not me, but his friends in general.* Lewis didn't respond straight away, but looked as if he was giving the question some thought. *Please let there be something holding him here*, Cleo thought.

"Well, actually ..." Lewis began, suddenly looking as if he'd made up his mind about something.

Cleo smiled at him encouragingly. *Say it, Lewis,* she thought. *Say there's something here you need to stay for. Say there's someone you need to stay for.*

"... actually, you're right, there's nothing

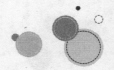

holding me here," Lewis finished. "I'm out of here." And with that, Lewis got to his feet decisively. "Thanks Cleo," he added, looking down at her briefly before turning and walking away.

Cleo was glad Lewis didn't look back. For the second time that day, she was grateful that he wasn't around to see her reaction to his words. *Maybe I've got Lewis all wrong*, she thought. *Maybe he doesn't care about me in the way I thought he did. If he can make a decision like this so easily, then maybe I've been stupid to think he'd want to stay here because of me. One way or the other, this means that Emma and Rikki and I are on our own as far as Denman's concerned. Lewis is under her spell and I've got to find a way to break it … but how?*

Chapter 11

Cleo's heart thumped in her chest as she leaned against the laboratory door. *This is my only chance*, she thought. *If I can just find out what Denman's really up to and convince Lewis that he's wrong about her, then maybe he'll stay. All I've got to do is get in there …*

She took a deep breath and opened the laboratory door. With a huge sigh of relief, she looked around and saw that the lab was empty. "Phew!" she exhaled, catching her breath and trying to slow her heartbeat.

Silently, and with a distinct feeling she'd been through all this before, she closed the door behind her and crept across to the other side of the room. Denman's laptop was sitting open on one of the bench tops and Cleo made

her way over to it and sat down. *Now,* she thought, *let's see what Dr Baywatch Babe has* really *been up to.*

Cleo moved the computer's mouse slightly to switch the screensaver off and the display lit up in front of her instantly. A document was already open and Cleo began to read over it carefully, deliberately sounding out each word aloud to herself to be certain she didn't miss anything: "*Just Add Water: the Phenomenon of Spontaneous Cellular Mutation,*" she read. "Oh, no!"

With a jump, Cleo heard the lab door click open behind her. She quickly slammed the laptop shut and spun around in her chair. Facing her was Bruce, one of the marine park's security guards.

"Cleo!" he said, as if he was just as surprised to see Cleo as she was to see him. "What are *you* doing in here?"

"Oh ... just ... looking for a friend," Cleo answered in the most innocent voice she could muster. *I can't let him think I'm up to anything*, she thought.

"Sorry, this is off limits," Bruce told her. "Dr Denman's orders. They're moving a lot of expensive equipment out of here today."

"Oh," Cleo said, getting up from the chair and walking hastily towards the door. "Right."

"And Cleo," Bruce added, just as Cleo squeezed past him through the door. "Don't let me catch you back here."

Cleo smiled as sweetly as she could, put her head down and marched quickly down the ramp towards the research pool. She had seen enough anyway – that document on Denman's laptop could only mean one thing. Denman still had her DNA sample and was doing research on it for a scientific paper. The only thing on her mind now was getting to

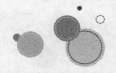

Lewis as fast as she could. She had to tell him that Denman still had the sample. He *had* to know what she was really like before he went traipsing across the other side of the world with her.

Chapter 12

Sitting in the Juice-Net Café with Lewis opposite her, Cleo couldn't have been more frustrated. She could have *screamed* with frustration if only there weren't so many people around. It was the look of utter disbelief on Lewis's face as he sat listening to her that was making her so mad. No matter how many times she told him what she'd seen on Denman's laptop, he just didn't want to believe it.

As soon as she'd told Rikki and Emma about the article, they'd realized how important it was, but when Lewis arrived at the Juice-Net Café and she'd begun telling him, all he did was immediately start lecturing her about how she didn't know what she was looking at. It was infuriating. *Maybe if I just kick him under the table*, she thought, *that'll knock some sense into him …*

"How many times do I have to tell you, it looked like an article for a scientific journal or something," she said instead. "It's the same stuff as you keep blabbing about, Lewis. It proves she's still got the DNA sample. It was in a little white slide box."

"Well, Lewis?" Emma asked, pursing her lips together expectantly.

"She *wouldn't*," Lewis said, leaning back in his chair almost smugly.

"It looked like she'd been studying it, doing tests." Cleo added hotly.

"She's *not* like that," Lewis said, shaking his head and leaning forward across the table again for extra emphasis.

Rikki sighed in frustration. She'd told Cleo that she'd be wasting her time trying to convince Lewis there was a dark side to Denman, but Cleo had insisted on giving him a chance. "Time to face facts, Romeo," she told Lewis from across the table.

"*Facts*?" Lewis snapped back at her, "you don't *have* any facts. Cleo, you read a bit of an article you don't understand."

"I understand enough to know it's the same stuff *you* say," Cleo replied adamantly, folding her arms defensively as she said it. *Why is he treating me like I'm an idiot?* she thought. *I don't deserve this! Not from Lewis, of all people.*

"So?" Lewis argued. "Maybe I've influenced her thinking. I have a very forceful personality."

"Ha!" Rikki snorted.

"Why do you think she wants me on her research trip?" Lewis added, ignoring Rikki's laugh. "Did it ever occur to you that there might be a reason? Like … like she values my opinion?"

"And your mopping," Rikki suggested sarcastically.

Lewis glared at Rikki silently. This was about as much as he could take. The fact that

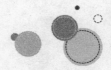

his friends no longer seemed to trust him was one thing, but being openly ridiculed by them was another thing altogether. Without waiting another second, Lewis hustled himself out of the booth and skulked off towards the door, pushing the beads aside and almost bumping into someone coming in.

An uncomfortable silence descended over the girls' table, none of them wanting to be the first to say just how drastic their situation now was. Not only did they now know that Denman still had the sample, but any chance they had had of Lewis helping them out was now clearly gone.

"He's lost it," Rikki whispered. "Totally."

Emma nodded. "We've got to find a way to get into that lab," she said thoughtfully. As far as she was concerned, there was only one way out of this mess and that was to fix it themselves. It was obvious to her that Lewis was a lost cause. There was no way he was going to believe what Cleo had seen, so their

only option was to get that slide back and, with any luck, have Denman sailing off into the sunset before she even realized the slide was gone. And if that meant sneaking into Denman's lab one more time, then that was the plan.

"Ah, correction," Cleo said. "You guys have to. I'm going to lose my job if I get caught in that place again."

Right, thought Emma determinedly, seeing the sense in what Cleo was saying, *there's no point in Cleo losing her job if we can avoid it. Rikki and I will just have to do this on our own.*

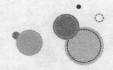

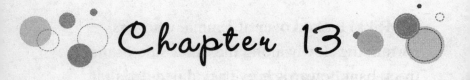
As she swam through the water with Emma beside her, Rikki wished that Cleo was with them. Cleo knew the marine park much better than she or Emma did, and if they didn't find their way through to the right area of the park in time, they'd miss their opportunity to catch Denman before all the equipment was packed onto the boat. They knew that the boat was due to leave tomorrow morning, so there wasn't any time for missed opportunities. This was their only chance.

Still, even without Cleo there, Rikki was confident that she and Emma would get the job done. All they had to do was find the gate that led from the open waters into the marine park pools and they could swim the rest of the way through to the dolphin research pool undetected.

Rikki looked over at Emma, who was swimming slowly along the other side of the rock bank towards her. They'd decided that if they headed roughly in the direction of the marine park, then split up and swam towards one another, sooner or later one of them would come across the gate they knew must be there. Unfortunately, it looked as if Emma wasn't having any luck, and they were only a short distance away from each other now. Sensing that perhaps she'd overlooked something, Rikki gave a swift flick of her tail and doubled back towards a small cleft in the rock bank that she hadn't investigated thoroughly enough. Sure enough, when she swam in for a closer look, hidden behind some straggly kelp was a small iron gate. *Bingo!* she thought as she looked up and beckoned Emma over.

Of course, the gate was locked. Emma looked around, hoping to find another way in. Instead

she found what looked like a large lever. She swam up to it and tried her luck. Sure enough, one tug on the lever and the gate opened with a watery thud.

Rikki helped Emma to swing the gate open just enough for them both to swim through, then closed it again, latching it shut – they wanted to get in, but they didn't want to be responsible for any of the park's dolphins getting out!

The tunnel on the other side of the gate was only a short one, and before long they were swimming along the bottom of the marine park's various pools, hugging the sides and keeping to the shaded areas. Compared to the ocean waters they were used to swimming in, the pools were only shallow and they didn't want to risk being seen. They swam from one pool to the next until they found one with only a single dolphin swimming happily about. *This must be the research pool*, Rikki thought.

Cleo said there would only be one dolphin in it. One dolphin named Marge. She smiled as the dolphin swam up to her and rubbed its tail against her own tail playfully. *Sorry Marge, but playtime's for later. Right now we've got work to do.*

Suddenly, Rikki felt Emma grab her hand and motion towards a small pier that jutted out above them. Through the shimmering surface of the water, Rikki could vaguely make out the shape of Dr Denman walking up and down the pier as she piled crates of equipment near the edge. Rikki smiled. They'd made it in time. Giving Emma a quick nod, they both pushed off with their tails from the bottom of the pool and glided up towards the surface, their heads emerging silently from the water just as they heard a familiar voice in the distance.

"Dr Denman," they heard Lewis call out, approaching from the other end of the pier.

"Lewis," Denman answered, looking up

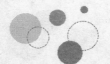

from the boxes she was sorting through.

"Packing already?" he asked, stopping just above where Emma and Rikki had positioned themselves in the water below. They could just see bits and pieces of Lewis as they looked up through the narrow gaps in the timber pier, but could hear him and Denman speaking quite clearly.

"Well, I want us to get an early start tomorrow morning, Lewis," Denman answered.

"Um, yeah," Lewis started to say, taking off his hat and pushing his hair back nervously. "Listen, can you be straight with me about something?"

Rikki and Emma exchanged a questioning glance between them. *What's Lewis up to?* Rikki thought. He only ever does that hat thing when he's anxious about something.

"Anything," Denman answered without hesitation as she picked up another box – Rikki saw that it was labelled 'slides' – and carried it

down to the end of the pier.

Lewis looked at Denman for a moment, as if he was deciding whether or not he really wanted to say what he was about to say, then boldly straightened his shoulders and spoke.

"Did you hold on to that slide of mine?" he asked.

"Yes," said Denman matter-of-factly.

"It's not like you have to pretend ... did you say *yes*?" Lewis stammered disbelievingly. He'd expected her to deny taking the slide and had been ready to launch into apologies and a full explanation of how she shouldn't take the accusation as a sign that he didn't trust her. But now that she'd said yes, he was lost for words.

"Yes, I did," Denman replied, again without a hint of hesitation. "It's right here with all of our Mako slides. And I'm hoping one day, Lewis, you'll be a little more forthcoming about where you got it."

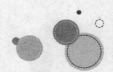

"Um ..." Lewis muttered, not really knowing how to react to such an open admission of theft. Emma and Rikki pulled themselves up a bit closer to the pier. They didn't want to miss a word of what Denman had to say. They were both just as shocked as Lewis was to hear Denman admit she'd taken the slide from him. Of course, they knew she had, based on what Cleo had told them about the article she'd seen. But they had never expected Denman to just come right out and say it like that. And to be so unapologetic about it too! Not only that, but now they knew that the slide was only metres from their grasp. *If only there was some way to get it*, thought Rikki. *Then this whole fiasco would be over.*

"Lewis," they heard Denman say. "You've got something extraordinary here – cells that completely change their molecular structure on contact with water."

Keeping a close eye on Denman, Rikki

began to lift herself out of the water and reach up towards the pile of boxes Denman had stacked at the end of the pier. If she could time it just right …

"Sounds impossible," Lewis said blankly, seeing Rikki's hand reaching up over the pier from out of the corner of his eye.

"It *is* impossible," Denman replied. "But here it is," she added, turning around and gesturing towards the slide box. Lewis's heart skipped a beat, but thankfully, before Denman had fully turned, Rikki's hand darted back down out of sight. "I can't explain it," Denman went on, leaning down towards the slide box to pick it up. "We need to do a lot more tests."

"You stole it from me," Lewis said, causing Denman to face him. Rikki saw her chance and reached for the slide box once more, but she wasn't quick enough. As soon as she was out of the water far enough to make a grab for the box, she saw Denman start to turn

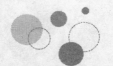
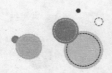

back towards it. She had no choice but to slip back into the water as quickly and silently as she could. The slide box was as good as gone. It might as well have been in the Galapagos Islands already as far as Rikki was concerned. She let out a frustrated scream deep under the water, then, not wanting to miss anything that Denman and Lewis said to each other, flicked her tail and swam back to the surface.

"Lewis, I'm sorry I deceived you," Denman said as Rikki emerged. She had already picked up the slide box and was standing directly in front of Lewis, looking him straight in the eye with an earnest look. "But I have no intention of ripping you off," she went on. "Why do you think I want you on this trip with me?"

'Is it the charm?" Lewis asked hopefully.

"Lewis, do you think you could get more samples like this?" Denman asked.

"What about trust?" Lewis asked, ignoring Denman's question.

"You can trust me to be a good scientist," she answered, putting her arm around Lewis's shoulder as she spoke. "Like I said, I believe in your talent."

"I appreciate that," Lewis said, turning and heading back towards the path around the research pool.

"Are you still coming tomorrow?" Denman said as he started to walk away.

"Can I have a look at your research so far?" Lewis called back, stopping to wait for her answer.

"Of course," Denman answered.

"Then I wouldn't miss it for the world," Lewis said as he walked away.

Rikki and Emma had heard enough. Lewis was as good as gone and they still weren't any closer to getting the slide back. And as far as either of them could see, they had just missed their last chance. They both slipped

silently back into the pool and swam wearily out towards the open water, neither of them daring to utter a single word. They were both absolutely certain of the catastrophe that lay ahead of them but neither wanted to say it out loud.

Lewis though, wasn't so certain about things. When Denman had admitted to taking the slide, his entire opinion of her had been instantly flipped upside down. No longer did he see her as the gorgeous genius who was going to sweep him away and steer him towards scientific greatness. Instead, he was beginning to see her as an opportunistic thief, someone he wanted to spend as little time with as possible. When she'd put her arm around him and told him he could trust her to be a good scientist, Lewis had felt disgusted. He knew that if she'd done the same thing ten minutes earlier he would've lapped up such a show of affection, but after hearing that she had betrayed him, her arm around him almost made him sick.

And this was the woman he was about to spend six months with in a research lab on the other side of the world? No, Lewis wasn't so certain about things at all – he knew he had some thinking to do.

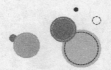

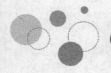

Chapter 14

The next morning, Cleo met up with Emma and Rikki in the park just as the sun began to shine its first rays over the horizon. The day was clear and crisp, with just a hint of chillness in the breeze. Standing on the path that led out towards the Marina, Cleo looked out at the ocean and pulled her jacket close around her. It didn't make her feel any warmer, but then she knew it wasn't the breeze that was making her feel cold. Emma and Rikki, sitting on the park bench beside her, seemed to be leaning in towards one another for comfort as well.

"I didn't sleep a wink last night," Cleo said miserably, sitting down beside her friends.

"Me neither," Rikki and Emma replied in unison.

"You *do* realize she'll eventually get it out of him, don't you?" Emma asked with an air of

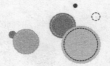

resignation, pulling her sleeves over her hands and then burying them under her armpits.

"What?" Cleo asked gloomily.

"Where the DNA came from," Emma explained with a definite note of annoyance. *What else could I mean?* She didn't mean to be annoyed with Cleo, but the whole situation was just so awfully frustrating. She'd been sure that their plan to get the slide back yesterday would work, but when she'd seen Denman reach out to take the slide box almost out of Rikki's grasp, her heart had sunk just as she and Rikki had sunk back to the bottom of the pool. It was hopeless. She might have spent the whole night lying awake and thinking up new and elaborate plans to break into Denman's lab, but she knew she wasn't going to go through with any of them. The way their luck was going, she'd end up being arrested or something, and where would that leave them? Although she had to admit that it didn't seem like things could possibly get any worse than they were now.

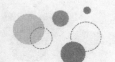
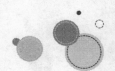

"We have to get that slide back," Rikki mumbled, staring off into the distance as if she too was trying to think up a new plan to get it back.

"Lewis wouldn't sell us out completely," Cleo said as optimistically as she could. "Would he?"

"Stop having so much faith in human nature," Rikki snapped angrily, turning to face Cleo. "He already *has* sold us out. You're the only one who doesn't think so. Why is that?"

"I just don't believe it," Cleo answered dully. *He can't have sold us out*, she thought. *Not Lewis. Not my Lewis. I just can't believe he would do something like that. But from what Emma and Rikki saw at the research pool, it sounds like he just stood there and accepted the fact that she'd stolen the sample from him. It just doesn't make sense! The Lewis I know wouldn't put up with that and the Lewis I know definitely wouldn't agree to spend six months*

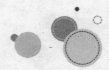

with someone he knew to be that deceitful.

As far as Cleo could see, there was something seriously wrong with the whole situation. It just didn't add up. The Lewis she knew would not do such a thing. All she knew was that Lewis was her friend and if Lewis had ever needed friends, he needed them now.

"Lewis is ... our friend," Cleo said with an air of decisiveness as she stood up and started to walk down the path towards the Marina.

"Where are you going?" Emma asked as Cleo started walking away.

"I'm going to go and talk to Lewis," Cleo called back over her shoulder without stopping. She had the look of someone who had made up her mind and there was no way anyone could talk her out of it. "Even if it is for the last time," she added.

Rikki and Emma stared after her, neither of them knowing quite what to make of Cleo's new determination. Suddenly, Cleo stopped,

turned and called back to them. "Well?" she shouted expectantly.

Emma looked at Rikki questioningly, as if to say, 'what choice have we got?' They both knew it was a long shot. After all, there was every chance that Lewis and Denman's boat had already left, but it was better than no chance at all. Hurriedly, they grabbed their things from the bench and ran to catch up with Cleo. If they were quick, maybe they could just make it in time.

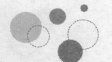

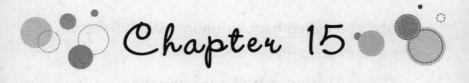

Chapter 15

Racing along through the Marina and rounding the last corner towards the mooring where they'd last seen Denman's boat, the girls came to an abrupt halt. The jetty was empty. Still out of breath from the run through the park, they all looked up together to see the boat's silvery wake trailing off towards the horizon, pulling away from them swiftly and taking with it the last of their hopes.

"That's her boat," Emma sighed despondently, stamping her feet in frustration.

"Come on," Cleo said, still with the same air of determination she'd shown at the park. "If anybody can catch her, we can." She started unlacing her shoes, as if she planned on diving straight into the water without another thought.

"Wait," Rikki said, grabbing Cleo's arm

gently. "I think that might defeat the purpose of all the secrecy, don't you?"

"Oh," Cleo answered, realizing the recklessness of what she was about to do – swimming right up to Denman's boat and leaping out of the water tails and all. "You're right, sorry. But are we just going to let him go like this?" Cleo added, looking out to sea and watching the boat disappear, knowing that she was watching Lewis slip out of her life along with it.

"Like what?" Lewis's voice suddenly asked from behind them.

"Well, you're just sailing away without saying … Lewis!" Cleo shouted delightedly, turning to see Lewis smiling back at her. "You didn't go!"

"Keen observation, Cleo; very, very good," Lewis replied casually. He was leaning against the jetty's side-railing, his hands in his pockets as if he'd been standing there the whole time.

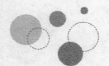

Still smiling, he pulled the slide from his pocket and held it up in front of the girls like a magician with a new card trick.

"You got the slide back!" Emma squealed happily.

"And she didn't suck you in?" Rikki asked, sounding as if she wasn't quite willing to abandon all of her suspicions just yet. She still had her doubts about whether or not Lewis was free of Denman's spell.

"What, are you *serious*?" Lewis answered. "You think I'd buy that stuff about being a good scientist? *Please*."

"What about her records? All the stuff I saw?" Cleo asked nervously. She couldn't quite believe what she was seeing and hearing. Just when she thought that all her worst nightmares had come true, it was as if she'd woken up to find that the world she loved was just as she had left it. Lewis was still there and apparently, Denman had meant nothing to him. It all

seemed too good to be true, but it *was* true.

"When she opens the file, I think she'll find it's recently been erased – oops," Lewis said, earning himself a smile from Rikki, who was starting to believe that everything might just be okay after all. "No, I don't think the good Doctor and I are a team any more, guys."

Cleo looked at Lewis proudly. She knew what a big decision it must have been for him to abandon Denman's research offer. *That job was everything he's ever wanted,* she thought. *And he gave it all away for us – to protect our secret. I really am lucky to have a friend like him. And he still looks cute in that hat!*

"It's good to have you back, Lewis," she said. And then, without thinking about it, she reached out to give Lewis a hug. Or at least, she started out trying to give him a hug, but somewhere between Lewis reaching his arms out towards her and her taking another step towards him, the hug somehow turned

awkwardly into a cross between a high-five and a handshake. Cleo smiled to herself. Hug or no hug, it was still good to have Lewis back – *her Lewis*, just the way she liked him.

"Thank you," Lewis said shyly. He had no idea that doing the right thing could be so embarrassing.

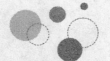